Twin Trouble

Twin Trouble

Iridescent Toad Publishing

Iridescent Toad Publishing.

First edition. ISBN 978-1-913779-52-8

Chapter One

"Pass it up here!" I shouted.

The boys scuffled around the ball at the other end of the playground.

"Over here! I'm right near the goal!" I called.

Still nobody passed the ball to me.

"Fine then, I'll do it myself," I huffed under my breath.

I ran to the other end of the playground and shoved my way into the scuffle of lads who were struggling to get the ball over to the goal side of the concrete pitch. It wasn't long before I nudged past a few more people and then BAM! I kicked the ball with so much force that it landed straight in the goal.

"Gooooooooal," I screeched at the top of my voice.

I ran round in celebration. I couldn't celebrate like the boys though. I couldn't lift my shirt over my head and run around with my arms in the air with everyone able to see my belly button. I was the only girl who played football in our year group. The other girls in year six sometimes sat around the pitch as they half watched us play in between plaiting their hair. They never joined in though. I had always found them a bit boring for that.

"Grace," I said as I ran up to my sister who was sitting with the other girls. "Did you see that goal I just scored?"

I scuffed my shoes against the pavement as I spoke to her. I would need a new pair soon. They were tattered and muddy, but I didn't care.

"Well done, Liv," said Grace as she looked up at me.

I noticed that her eyes looked a little tearful.

"Hey, what's wrong?" I asked.

I wanted to get back to the game but I was more worried about Grace now.

"Play on," I called across to the boys gathered around the football.

I sat down next to Grace and picked at one of the scabs on my knees.

"I'm all yours now," I said to her. "What's wrong?"

"I'm just worried."

"About what?"

"All kinds of things."

"Yeah, but it's break time," I said, a little confused. "You shouldn't be worrying now. You should be playing and having fun. Why don't you come and play football with me?"

"You know I don't like football," Grace said with a sigh.

"I know, I know," I said playfully in mock exaggeration. "Sometimes I swear we're not even twins. Anyway, what is it that you're so worried about?"

"Lots of things," said Grace. "I'm worried about Dad. I'm worried about the exams that are coming up."

"Yeah, but you can't do anything about either of those things at the moment. You can't go home and talk to Dad – and even if you could, there's nothing you can say to cheer him up anyway. As for the exams, they're *ages* away. Thinking about them now won't do you any good. Why don't you cheer up? Go off and play hairdressers with Jenna or something?"

"No," said Grace. "I like sitting here and watching you. Are you still winning the game by the way?"

"I don't know," I said as I stood up to call out across the playground. "Oi! What's the score? Are we still winning?"

"I don't know," Colin shouted.

"Well, that's silly," I said to no one in particular as I went to find out.

I marched across the pitch to the huddle of boys who were all standing around the ball, which was now in a sorry (and flattened!) state.

"What the flip has happened to that?" I asked.

"Gary punctured it," Colin said solemnly.

"What?! Why?" I asked.

"Because he'd had enough of the game and

decided that we should all stop," said Colin, throwing his hands in the air in frustration.

"We'll see about that," I said.

I could see Gary and his mates at the other end of the small playground. They were leaning against the wall and looking very pleased with themselves. Gary stood in the middle; on one side of him was Craig and on the other was Tom. Both of them were smaller than Gary but were just as troublesome.

I wasn't scared of them. *Nobody* scared me. I started marching towards them, rolling up the sleeves of my jumper as I did so.

"Oi!" I shouted. "What do you think you're doing coming over and popping our ball like that?"

"Felt like it," Gary said, not even bothering to give a decent answer.

"You'd better go inside and ask if we can have another ball out here to play with," I said as I walked closer to him.

He looked like he didn't care. Craig and Tom just stood there sniggering and looking impressed by how difficult Gary was being.

"Off you go then," I said. "Go inside and get us another ball."

By now, Gary and I were square up next to each other. He was bigger than me but I didn't care.

"Make me," he said.

I know I shouldn't have done it, but I was so annoyed by that point that before he knew it was coming, I put my arms out and shoved Gary against the wall. Craig and Tom backed away from the whole thing. Gary started shoving me back but I used all my strength and gave as good as I got. As we moved around the small area of the playground trying to push each other over, I could see out of the corner of my eye that everyone who had been playing football was now gathered around to watch. Even the girls who had been playing quietly at the side of the pitch were stood looking worried.

Neither of us wanted to back down, but through the crowd of kids who had gathered to gawp at us, we heard a whistle being blown. It caught our attention straight away. As we looked up to see what was going on, I felt the force of Gary's strength against me suddenly stop. Mrs Greenwood was walking towards us with a determined expression on her face.

"What's going on here?" she demanded.

Nobody spoke; nobody wanted to dob us in or to get involved. After all, most of the kids huddled around us had only been watching.

I could feel my heart thudding against my chest as Mrs Greenwood motioned for Gary and I to walk behind her. Even though I was used to getting in trouble, I still hated how it felt.

As Gary and I followed behind Mrs Greenwood, we looked at each other sheepishly. I was still annoyed at him for having popped our ball and for how he'd tried to act all tough about it. It would have been easier if we'd both managed to calm down earlier though.

Before we turned the corner to Mrs Greenwood's office, I quickly turned around to look back at the crowd of kids who were still watching us. At the front was Grace. She was looking straight at me and she looked so worried. As she bit at her already-chewed nails, she looked like she was about to cry.

I hated the thought of Grace being upset, and so I gave her a thumbs-up signal – really big and bold to show her that everything was going to be fine.

Chapter Two

The smell of coffee and new pencils in Mrs Greenwood's office was overwhelming. Gary and I sat there in silence as she plonked herself down on the chair behind her side of the desk. She was a thin woman but she moved with force and determination. I tried to distract myself from the situation by wondering what she would look like as a skeleton. If she'd sat down with any more force, maybe her bones would have snapped. I'd hate that to happen to anyone of course, but in not looking forward to being shouted at, I was keen to distract myself.

"What was that all about?" she demanded in a thick Scottish accent as she looked across at Gary, and then to me.

Neither of us said anything. It didn't seem wise to.

"Look," said Mrs Greenwood, slightly raising her voice. "We can sit here all afternoon or we can get to the bottom of this. Either way, we *will* talk about this. In less than a year you'll be going up to secondary school and this sort of behaviour won't wash there. Not only that, but you could both find yourselves in worse trouble. What if someone bigger and stronger had come along?"

"I hadn't thought of that," I blurted out, not really thinking about what I was saying.

"And that's the problem, Olivia," said Mrs Greenwood. "You don't *think* before you *do*. You can be very impulsive at times. You should be more like Grace. Why can't you take a leaf out of her book? Besides, she looks up to you and you should try to set a good example."

Grace was actually only younger than me by a few minutes but now didn't feel like the time to mention that to Mrs Greenwood – her cheeks were starting to go red. Perhaps she was genuinely frustrated.

"As for you, Gary," Mrs Greenwood continued. "You've had so many fights this year. It needs to stop and it needs to stop *now*. When you get to secondary school it could get more serious. You're going to be a young man soon, and before you know it!"

"Olivia started it," said Gary.

"Oh yeah? And how did I start it?" I snapped. "You were the one who popped our ball!"

"Yeah," Gary retorted. "And you were the one who started pushing me."

"Ah," said Mrs Greenwood. "So now we're getting somewhere. Is it true, Gary, that you popped their football?"

Gary didn't answer.

"Of course it is," I said. "Ask the other kids."

"Thank you Olivia," said Mrs Greenwood as she put her hand up to silence me. "Let Gary speak please."

Still Gary said nothing.

"Come on, Gary," said Mrs Greenwood. "I'll find out somehow so now's *your chance* to tell me."

"Yeah, ok. I popped the ball," Gary said with a shrug.

He didn't look bothered. He was always doing stuff like this.

"And is that why you started pushing him?" Mrs

Greenwood asked as she looked at me.

"Yes," I said.

It didn't make sense to deny what had happened. All of the other kids had seen it anyway. Besides, the sooner we could get out of here, the sooner we could go back to playing outside – that's if there was even anything left of break time.

"Hmmm, ok," said Mrs Greenwood as she fumbled around for something in her desk drawer. "I'm going to write a letter home for both of you. I'll give it to you both at the end of the day and I expect a signed slip to be returned to me tomorrow morning. I want to know that they have been read. Agreed?"

I hated it when Mrs Greenwood asked if we agreed with something. This was a word that she had often used when concluding a telling-off. It didn't make sense though. I didn't want to agree to what she was saying but I had no choice. If it were up to me, I wouldn't even take a letter home. Why would I want Dad to know that I'd been in trouble? He had enough on his mind. All the same though, I didn't want to get into *more* trouble.

I slouched in my chair as I thought about how Grace didn't need this either. I was used to getting in trouble but I hated how it made her feel when I did. She wanted to be good. She had always been what other people call "the quiet one". She was never quiet with me though. I promised myself that I would apologise to her later. I hated the thought that my actions often caused her to worry.

As I looked down at my shoes against the grey carpet of Mrs Greenwood's office, I wished so hard that there was something I could do to make Grace be ok. Not just Grace, but Dad too.

Chapter Three

"Not another one, Liv," said Dad, shaking his head.

The three of us – Dad, Grace and I – had just had a lovely dinner together. I'd handed him the letter from school immediately afterwards. I had told Grace that we should keep quiet about the whole thing until after dinner, just to give us some time to relax for a bit. Grace had looked worried but as always, she agreed to follow along with what I thought was best.

"Sorry Dad," I said.

Grace still had a few chips on her plate. She pushed them around a bit with her fork, trying to keep them away from the small blob of tomato ketchup that she'd decided she didn't fancy anymore. Or maybe she was just trying to look busy because she didn't want to say anything.

"What's it for this time then?" Dad said with a sigh as he opened the envelope.

His eyes quickly scanned over Mrs Greenwood's handwritten scrawl from earlier. He was probably more familiar with her handwriting than some of the kids in her class were.

"Is all of this true, Liv?" Dad asked.

Dad had always been kind, and keen to give me the benefit of the doubt. He was always patient and he never shouted. Whenever I got in trouble for something at school, he just looked sad. That alone was enough to make me feel bad though.

"Yeah, it's true," I said, knowing that Mrs Greenwood wasn't one to mince her words. "I'm sorry Dad."

"Aww Liv," he said, the disappointment in his voice entirely obvious. "When's it going to stop, eh? Come on girl, try a bit harder. Not just for me, but for Grace."

Grace still didn't say anything. She was still pushing the chips on her plate around, even though they had probably had a good tour of every part of it by now – several times over!

I didn't know how to answer Dad's question. I *wanted* to be good. I *wanted* to be able to promise him that I'd stop getting into trouble. But could I make that kind of promise and truly stick to it? I wasn't sure.

"Here's the thing, Liv," Dad continued. "You're going to have to change your focus whether you like it or not. It's not long now until you've both got exams coming up, plus those extra ones that I've put you in for."

"I hate exams," I said. "Why should we have to do more of them?"

"Because you've both got the opportunity to go to a grammar school," said Dad. "Do you know how lucky that makes you? Most parts of the country got rid of them years ago, but there's one just down the road from here. I think it would be a missed opportunity not to at least *try* to get in there, don't you?"

"But *why*?" I asked, exasperated.

"Come on, Liv," said Dad. "We've been over this before. It's an opportunity. All I ask is that you *try*."

To be fair to Dad, we *had* been over this before – and quite a few times too! I didn't really care which secondary school I was going to end up at, just so long as I could stay with Grace. School would be rubbish without her. Not just that, but I always needed to know that she was ok. How would I be able to do that if she was all the way across town at a completely different school?!

The conversation that we'd had so many times about this had always gone along the lines of how Dad wanted us to have the best opportunity in life to do well. I'd always say that I wasn't worried about that. And Grace would always sit there quietly but say that she was happy to do the extra exams.

Grace had always enjoyed studying. I had never understood her for that. I had always found it so boring. What's interesting about remembering a load of stuff that you're not really that bothered about? Exams never asked interesting questions about stuff like football, or video games. The questions were always about stupid and boring things. Grace though, she had always been good at just keeping her head down and doing as she was told. Dad and the teachers at our primary school had been saying for ages that she'd do well at grammar school. It was me who they were more worried about.

"All I ask is that you try," Dad said again for the millionth time.

"Ok Dad," I said, looking him straight in the eyes.

"I'll try."

"You're my princesses," said Dad. "And I want you both to have the world."

Chapter Four

Grace and I sat in our room. She was drawing and I was playing a video game. Each time I took my eyes off the game for a bit to look up at what she was doing, her drawing had developed into something even prettier than the last time I'd looked. This time, she was working on a pretty piece with a flower on it. All of her pencils were lined up neatly to the side. Various shades of pink and green were organised so that she could do the shading and highlighting as she went along. I had never been very good at art, but I understood a little bit about it from what Grace had told me.

"Sorry about today," I said to Grace.

"It's ok," she said.

"Really?"

She often said that something was ok even when it wasn't. It didn't surprise me to hear her say it but there was a part of me that wanted to ask her if she *really* was ok with things.

"Come on," I said. "You looked so worried when you saw me being marched off to Mrs Greenwood's office."

"Yeah," said Grace. "But what was I supposed to do? Watching you get in trouble is never very nice, but it's not like there's anything I can do about it."

"Well of course it's not *nice*," I said. "It's not supposed to be *nice*. I guess by making a big thing of this stuff, the teachers are hoping that they can embarrass us into behaving."

"Then why don't you?" Grace asked.

It was a good question to be fair.

"I don't know," I said.

And even if I did know, I wasn't too sure about telling Grace. I knew that she was already upset about how things had been recently. I didn't want to make her more upset by telling her about all of the things that I sometimes struggled with.

"It's Mum, isn't it?" said Grace.

I turned off the video game I'd been playing. I didn't feel like playing it anymore.

"Come on," said Grace. "You can tell me. I'm sad too."

"Yeah, but you're not as shy about showing it," I said honestly, albeit a little defensively.

"Well, I guess I'm not," said Grace. "But that doesn't mean that I'm finding things easy. It doesn't mean that I'm finding them harder than you either. I don't know because you don't always want to talk to me about this stuff."

I paused for a moment. After seeing how upset Grace had been today, I felt that the least I could do was open up to her, even if only a bit.

"Yeah," I said. "I'm still sad. I probably just do a better job of hiding it than you do."

Grace looked a bit offended at that.

"That's not to say that because I'm hiding it, I'm handling it better," I jumped in quickly.

I didn't want Grace to think that I thought I was handling things better than she was. I didn't think I was anyway. We were both sad and we were both showing it in different ways. Mum had been gone for nearly two years now and the way it felt inside, even though I was perhaps managing to cover it up on the outside, well, it never got any easier.

I felt like I was going to cry but I didn't want to. I had cried in front of Grace plenty of times before, but not much over this. I wanted to be strong not just for me, but for her. I had decided a long time ago that if I looked sad about things, or worried, or weak, it would just make her even more upset. And I didn't want to do that. I wanted Grace to be happy. I had even got into fights with other girls at school before when they'd been giving Grace a hard time. Grace had told me that she'd wished I hadn't but still, if I didn't defend my sister, then who would? Dad had always been a bit weedy, a bit nerdy. It's probably why he was so keen for us to get into grammar school. And without Mum around to march into school to tell the teachers what for, then well, I saw it as more important than ever that *I* was there for Grace.

"You're crying," said Grace.

"No I'm not," I insisted. "It's just that I put too much vinegar on my chips."

"Liar," Grace said, a gentle laugh escaping.

She knew me better than anyone. I'd never liked vinegar that much.

"It's ok to be sad," she said, putting down the pencil in her hand. "I'm sad every day. I wish you would tell me when you feel sad. At least that way, we could be sad together. Not that that's a good thing, but you know what I mean."

"I understand," I said. "You're saying that you don't want to feel that you're on your own with it."

"Yes!" Grace said firmly, as if the penny had only just dropped for me. "Pretending that you're not sad won't bring Mum back."

It was a good point. Towards the end of Mum's life, we were nine years old. When talking to Grace and I, the nurses had used words like "forever sleep" to describe what was happening. We'd heard Dad talking with them though, and we knew what they meant – especially when Dad had used words like "the big C" whilst talking about how much he hated cancer and why did Mum have to have it.

"Yeah, ok. I'm crying," I said to Grace.

There was no point in lying about it. Tears were falling down my cheeks now.

Grace stood up to put the picture she was working on flat on her bed. I knew she'd work on it later because she was always meticulous with her art. She really cared about it and I loved how the walls in our room sparkled with the castles and princesses she'd coloured in with glitter gel pen.

With her art and pencils safe and neatly aligned on the bed, Grace came back to sit down with me on the floor and gave me a big hug. She didn't need to say anything to me and I didn't need to say anything to her. She knew how I was feeling. As she gave me a tight and reassuring squeeze, it dawned on me that she must have known how I'd been feeling for a while.

I expected to feel her tears falling onto my shoulder, but there were none. After a while, I pulled away from our hug.

"You're not crying," I said.

"It's ok for you to be the one having a cry sometimes, you know," she said. "I'm here for you as much as you're here for me. You're not allowed to forget that."

I smiled at Grace. Although I usually did most of the talking for both of us, there were times where she knew just what to say with just a few little words.

Chapter Five

The next day at school, I'd already made a promise to myself that I would hang out with Grace and nobody else. I had told Grace about this the night before after we'd talked some more. I wanted to stay out of trouble so badly. Not only was this very much to Grace's approval, but she was also happy to hear that I wanted to follow along after her. For her, it would make a nice change from sitting on the sidelines, watching me while I played football.

Grace had often sat and watched me play football with the boys. She wasn't a tomboy herself but she often felt more at ease following me around rather than going off with the other girls in our class. They could be really mean to each other at times. I had never thought much of hanging out with them. Even when Grace did, she was never far away from me. The teachers had encouraged us to mix with the other kids a bit more at times, but we always chose to be near each other.

Grace was pleased that I wanted to hang out with her.

"No watching the football today then?" I asked jokingly.

"Definitely not," Grace said, beaming.

"What then?" I asked.

"I'm not sure actually," she said, sounding a bit lost.

"Do you remember when we used to pretend to be princesses?" I asked.

"Of course I do. It was fun."

"Yeah, Dad would call Mum his queen and they would both call us their princesses. We thought the idea was so fun that we would play together at being princesses – just down the other end of that playground," I said, pointing towards where the year two kids were playing. "I was the messy horrible princess who wanted to go out and look for wizards and witches so that I could learn to cast spells on evil goblins. You were the sweet and shy princess who wanted to stay in the castle, combing her sparkly long hair and waiting for a prince."

"I remember," said Grace. "Sometimes we'd pretend that we each had a unicorn."

"Except for when I wanted to have a dragon instead of a unicorn," I said.

We both laughed especially hard at this. Sometimes our imagination games had been so vivid. It was just the two of us together in our own special made-up world. It was often so immersive that we had ignored all of the other kids in the playground, even if they had asked to join in with all the fun that we were clearly having. I'd gallop around as if riding on my dragon, chasing after Grace as she elegantly tried to escape on her loyal unicorn.

We both paused in thought.

"What do you think we will be like when we go to secondary school together?" Grace asked.

"How do you mean?"

"Well, just hanging out together... Even if the other kids are weird, or boring, or horrible, we'll always have each other, won't we?"

"Of course we will," I said, not quite sure what Grace was getting at.

"It's just that if only one of us gets into grammar school, where will that leave us then?"

It was a good question. It hadn't even crossed my mind. Grace had always had a knack for thinking ahead.

"Well," I said, not sure what the answer was. "We could both hide on the day of the test. That way, we wouldn't have to take it."

The absurdity of the idea made me fall about laughing. Grace could only raise a forced smile though.

"I'm serious, Liv," she said. "What are we going to do? We *have* to sit the test because it means a lot to Dad. It would be really cruel to pretend that we'd done it when really we'd bunked off."

Grace was right. It meant a lot to Dad to see us both get into grammar school. I had never seen what all the fuss was about so I had never given it much thought. Dad had always valued studying. Even as an adult, he always had his head in his books. Working as a researcher for some of the universities had allowed him to indulge himself. I had never understood the appeal of it. Who would want to be cooped up indoors with their head in a book when they could be outside? Looking at the same four walls of a study room must be incredibly boring. I couldn't even stay in the school library for more than ten minutes without someone telling me to stop chatting.

"Yeah, yeah," I said. "We'll sit the boring test. The boring, smelly, poopy test."

"I'm serious, Liv," said Grace. "I wish you could be more serious sometimes."

"Hey!" I said, not quite offended but keen to defend my honour. "Remember what we both said last night?"

"Of course I do!"

"Well then. Just because I don't seem super serious all the time, it doesn't mean that I don't care. I want Dad to be happy. I want *you* to be happy. I want *us* to be happy."

"That means that you have to *try* on the exams then," Grace insisted.

"Who said I wouldn't?" I said, slightly offended now.

To be fair though, I hadn't made any plans to study. It hadn't crossed my mind to do it. Besides, I'm not psychic! How would I know what answers I'd need to memorise?!

"I'll try," I said, putting my face playfully right up to Grace's and trying to make her laugh.

It was a relief to be able to make Grace laugh when I needed to. It always lightened the mood and stopped her from being so overly serious and worried about things. I needed to make her laugh not only for that but because truthfully, I wasn't confident that I *could* try. I mean, how anyone could have any control over how they're going to do in an exam was beyond me. I didn't want to make a promise that I didn't even *understand* how to keep.

Chapter Six

"Come on, Liv," Grace said as she handed me my workbook. "Try to study."

"I did it earlier," I said, not quite convincingly enough.

Grace put her hands on her hips, giving me more attitude than she usually would. She must have really cared about this. Normally she wouldn't want to be the bossy one.

"Ok," I said with a heavy sigh.

Grace was already settled on the floor with her head in a book by the time I'd turned off my video game. Seeing that our bedroom was so quiet anyway, I figured that I may as well put a book in front of me. I picked one up from the pile that Grace had tactfully placed at the end of my bed.

Ugh! Maths! I thought to myself. *Stupid, boring, stinky maths.*

I looked down at Grace. She was so focused on what she was doing that she didn't even notice me watching her. I decided that the least I could do for her was to get comfortable on the bed. I bunched the duvet around me to make a soft fortress and then rested my back against the wall.

I opened the book on a random page. Percentages. *Ok, might as well stare at it in case something actually sinks in.*

It wasn't long before all of the words and numbers on the page started to blur together. I was bored by that point and although the book was open and I turned a page every so often for variety and to show Grace that at least I was trying, my mind was elsewhere. I started to daydream. *What would Mum say about all of this? Would she be overjoyed to see us doing well and getting into grammar school? Nah, she'd probably just be happy to still be here. What does it matter which school Grace and I end up going to as long as we get to stay together?*

My mind must have wandered off to somewhere far away.

"Wake up, Liv," said Grace as she put her face right up close next to mine. "Shall we have a break? I'm going downstairs to get some orange juice. Would you like some?"

"Yes please," I said. "And bring up some biscuits too."

"Lots of chocolate ones," Grace said, smiling as she gave me a hug.

As she thundered down the stairs, clearly still focused and keen to get back to studying after we'd had a break, I felt a bit guilty. Grace had always been so good at doing what was asked of her. Whether it was studying, tidying our room, or not answering back. Everyone thought of her as "the good one", no matter how hard they tried to – as they would always put it – "recognise us as individuals".

I went up to the bedroom window and looked outside at some of the younger kids playing in the street. I wanted to be in year four again; with no exams and no worries about moving up to secondary school. I laughed to myself at how funny the boys from next door looked as they wobbled about on their skateboards. They looked like they were trying to have a race but they wouldn't get very far without getting better at actually just skateboarding first. I wished I was out there skateboarding. I hadn't done it for a while because football was more my thing now. Anything would be better than being cooped up indoors, even though I was doing it for Grace.

"We've got chocolate bars and custard creams," Grace said as she came back into the room.

She gently placed the plate of biscuits on the floor so that we could sit down and share them.

"How long do we get to have this break for?" I asked.

"I think ten minutes should do. The sooner we get back to studying, the sooner we can say that we've done enough."

"So you don't actually *like* studying?"

"Not really," said Grace. "I guess it's just one of those things that has to be done and maybe it's not even about whether we like it or not."

I thought about it for a moment. I wasn't sure if Grace was making a good point or not.

"What's the point in doing things that you don't like?" I asked.

"I don't know," Grace said truthfully. "But once the exams are over and done with, we'll never have to do them again and then we can forget about them."

"I'd never thought about it like that," I said. "You're much better at thinking things through than I am. I guess all we need to do is get through this and then we can move on without having to worry about it anymore."

"Hopefully," said Grace. "Something like that."

Chapter Seven

Grace had been right. Just a few weeks later, the exams were over. Done and dusted. Whilst we were doing the exams, the time had dragged like crazy. Sometimes it had felt like I was guessing and other times it had felt like I was looking at the clock more than the actual paper that I was supposed to be writing on. It was great to be able to forget about the exams. Waiting to find out how we'd done felt like it was taking ages though.

One Saturday morning after breakfast, Dad sat us round the table. He had two envelopes in his hand that were marked with the grammar school logo on them.

"Now then," he said. "I think that inside these envelopes, there might be some very important news."

"Our exam results?" Grace asked, sounding very nervous.

"I think it's likely," said Dad. "I mean, it could just be some sort of advert or something and if it is, I'm sorry to have worried you. But if it is your exam results, I think it would be nice if we all opened them together, don't you?"

"I agree," I said. "Let's get this over and done with."

"Ok," said Dad. "Best of luck, girls. And remember, no matter what happens – no matter what it says on these letters – I am proud of you both."

"Can I open the envelopes, Dad?" I asked.

"No, Liv," he said firmly. "I want this to go smoothly... Right, let's get on with it."

If I had been allowed to open the envelopes, I would have torn into them like a lion tearing into a steak at the zoo (I'd seen it before on a nature programme on TV once, it had looked so frantic). Dad, although keen to get on with things, was far more methodical. He used the same posh-looking letter opener that he used for opening all of his post – whether something from one of the universities he worked for, or a phone bill.

Grace and I both watched him, completely focused

and waiting for the news.

A smile crept across Dad's face.

"Yep," he said, sounding overjoyed and reading from the letter aloud. "Linmore grammar school is looking forward to welcoming *Olivia Radley* in September."

He carried on reading the rest of the letter in a quick murmur, his eyes scanning across it so fast that it made him look almost robotic. Grace and I weren't interested in the small details though.

"That's brilliant," I chipped in. "If I've got in, then Grace must have got in too. Come on, you both know that Grace studied harder than me. The only reason I must have passed is because Grace practically chained me up in our room and *made* me study."

"Take some credit for your achievement though, Liv," said Dad. "This is yours. You've earned this."

I felt more relieved than anything. I didn't care about the exam results really, just so long as I knew that I would be going to the same secondary school as Grace.

Dad's eyes were already scanning across the letter

from the second envelope that he'd just opened.

"Dear Mr Radley," he read aloud. "We regret to inform you that *Grace Radley* has not met... oh."

His voice trailed off as he continued to read the letter quietly. He looked so upset that his face was almost grey.

"What is it?" I asked, bursting to know what was in the letter.

Dad turned to look at Grace.

"I'm really sorry, Gracie," he said to her. "But this letter says that you didn't get in."

Grace sat there in silence. She was probably shocked, or perhaps even a little embarrassed.

"That's ridiculous!" I piped up. "There must have been a mistake. If *I* managed to get in, then Grace should have *definitely* got in. What if the person who marked Grace's work was really horrible and mean and tight with giving a nice score? Or even worse! What if they mixed the two of us up? What if Grace was the one who really passed the exam and I was the one who didn't?"

Dad sighed and put his head in his hands. It took

him a while to look up at us.

"Did you put your name on the paper that you had to write your answers on?" Dad asked.

"Yes," I said.

Grace nodded.

"Well then," said Dad. "It is what it is."

"This is outrageous," I said, suddenly feeling very angry. "And it isn't fair. Grace needs to go to the same secondary school as me. It will be rubbish if we have to go to different ones. Who's going to stand up for Grace if she gets picked on? Who's going to be around to remind me not to get into fights?"

I felt like I was about to cry. I had always thought that Grace was smarter than me. She must be! How was it that I could get into grammar school and she couldn't? It didn't make any sense.

"Grace tried so hard," I shouted. "It should have been her who passed those stupid tests, not me."

"Were you nervous in the exams?" Dad spoke gently to Grace.

"Yes," she said. She was crying now.

"Some people who do well at school struggle with exams because they don't perform well under pressure," said Dad. "It's not the end of the world, Grace. I promise. All it means is that the next time you do an exam, the only way is up."

It was horrible to hear Dad say that to Grace. It was the sort of thing that he'd always said to me when I'd been naughty at school. It wasn't fair that Grace had to go through this, not after how hard she'd tried.

"If everyone passed every exam, there would be no point in doing them," said Dad.

Dad was good at being clever about these things. He had always been good at school and had gone to college and university. He had always been studious. It had always come so easily to him. Both he and Mum had always thought that Grace would be the one to follow in his footsteps.

The more Grace cried, the angrier I felt.

"It's not fair," I yelled. "This is so bloody stupid!"

"There's no need to swear, Liv," said Dad, annoyed but trying to keep his cool.

"I don't care," I shouted. "It's bloody, bloody, bloody stupid."

I stood up and gave Grace a huge cuddle as she sat slumped in her chair.

"Come on, Grace," I said, grabbing her hand tightly.

Grace was too upset to question my lead, even though it wasn't like her to follow along after me when I'd been arguing with Dad. I didn't care. I wasn't bothered about that. I just wanted Grace to be ok. I marched her along with me out of the kitchen. I wanted us to be away from those horrible letters. How dare *anyone* try to split us up?!

Chapter Eight

Once we were upstairs in our room and I'd slammed the door shut behind us, Grace threw herself onto her bed and sobbed into her pillow. I stayed quiet for a while. I had seen her cry loads of times before, but she didn't usually cry like this.

"Come on," I said as I handed her a tissue once she'd calmed down a little.

Grace took the tissue from me and then sat up. Her face was bright red and her eyes were puffy.

"Are you upset because you didn't get in, or because I did?" I asked, feeling a bit guilty.

"I'm not sure," Grace said, sniffing hard and trying not to start crying again.

"I'll tell you why I'm angry," I said. "I'm angry because I want to go to the same secondary school as you. I don't even care which one that is, just so long as I get to be with you. I don't want to go somewhere on my own, Grace. It will be so bloody boring."

"You probably shouldn't have sworn at Dad like that," said Grace.

"Hey!" I said, stomping my foot. "Whose side are you on here?"

"I'm not on anyone's side, Liv. It's just that Dad tried so hard to encourage us to do well in those exams, and even though I tried really hard, I still didn't manage to."

"Yeah, but you still tried," I said, keen to reassure her. "You said so yourself."

"It wasn't good enough though," said Grace as she started to cry a little again.

"It's not fair," I said. "You tried. You didn't just *pretend* try like I did. You actually *really tried.*"

"What do you mean? Pretend try?" asked Grace.

"Oh, you know," I said, suddenly desperate to play down what I'd just said. "Sometimes when I sat there with a book open trying to study, my mind wandered off somewhere else and I daydreamed about football and all kinds of other stuff. I *wanted* to try. Really I did. I wanted to try for you more than for me. I really don't care where I go to school, just so long as I get to stay with you."

"I'm pleased for you even though I'm sad for me," Grace said, reminding me of why Mrs Greenwood had once called her Gracious Grace.

An idea suddenly popped into my head.

"You know what," I said, full of determination. "I'm not going to go to that stupid school. I don't care about going there. I bet it's really rubbish anyway. I'm going to tell Dad that I'm not going because I want to go to the same school as you."

"But he tried really hard to encourage us. You might make him really sad if you tell him you're not going."

"I don't even care anymore," I said.

Truthfully, I did care. I didn't want to upset Dad. He had tried really hard. I wanted to see him happy. He had given it his all in trying to keep it all together after losing Mum. He had never been pushy with us and had always tried really hard to explain why it was important to him that we tried our best at school. Not only that, but he had looked so happy when he had read that I was being offered a place at grammar school.

"You do care, Liv," said Grace.

"Ok, yeah," I said. "I do care *a bit*. Of course I want Dad to be happy. But more than that, I can't bear the thought of you going to a different school all on your own. *I* don't want to go to a different school all on my own. I shouldn't have to. It's not fair."

"So what are you going to do?" Grace asked anxiously.

"Well," I said, trying to keep calm. "I could march downstairs right now and tell Dad that I'm angry and upset and that there's no way I'm going to go to that grammar school. But no, I'm going to calm down and talk to him later on today. I want to explain how we're both feeling without doing it in the heat of the moment."

"That's a good idea," Grace said, smiling a little. "If you go down there and talk to him now, you'll only end up swearing at him again."

"You see," I said. "And this is why I need to go to the same secondary school as you. Where would I be without you to remind me to keep my temper under control?"

We both looked at each other and felt a huge sense of relief. At least now we had a plan. We wanted to be together. We had always joked that one day, we would even be in the same old people's home together. Some twins aren't even identical – they look so different to each other that people are able to tell them apart. Not me and Grace though; not only did we look identical but we had made a pact that we would always be there for each other. It was a pact so strong that we'd never even really spoken to each other about it. It was something that had just been there from as long as we could both remember. We'd been through everything together. We were strong together. There was no way that I was going to let some stupid letter from some stupid school tear us apart like that. Not now, not ever.

Chapter Nine

I went downstairs to see Dad. He was still sat at the kitchen table nursing his cup of tea. It had probably gone cold by now. It looked like he hadn't moved since Grace and I had stormed off upstairs (well, since *I* had done the storming off – Grace had no choice but to tag along because I'd pulled her after me).

Dad looked like he was in a daze, his mind elsewhere.

"Are you ok?" I asked, almost forgetting that I was there to give him an apology.

"Oh, err, yes. I think so," he said.

I wasn't convinced. I pulled up a chair and sat right next to him at the table.

"You look really upset," I said. "I'm sorry for swearing at you. You were trying your best to be kind and encouraging and I just flew off on one.

I'm sorry."

"I understand," said Dad, never one to embrace confrontation. "You were upset. I can see that now."

"Yeah, but you're really upset too," I insisted.

The two of us sat there quietly for a moment, not wanting to upset one another with anything else. It made it so that I had to brace myself and take a deep breath before telling him what I needed to say.

"Dad," I said. "I'm not going to grammar school. If Grace isn't going, then neither am I."

"Is that really how you feel though?" Dad asked.

"Yes!" I insisted, a little annoyed that he'd even asked. "I want to go to the same school as Grace and the only way to make that happen is for me to go to the same secondary school that will take her."

"I see," said Dad. It sounded like he was carefully trying to take on board what I was saying.

"Well?" I asked expectantly.

"You might like it there," said Dad. "Honestly, Liv. There's an open evening there soon and I think you should at least go and take a look around to see what you make of it."

"Yeah, but that's not fair on Grace."

"Look," said Dad, exasperated. "It's not that the school that Grace will be going to is bad or that it won't be good for her. It's not about one school being worse than the other. It's about each of you getting the right education."

"Why are you so obsessed with education anyway?"

"Come on, Liv. You know I've had some good opportunities in life due to my own education. Without them, I might not have been able to keep working from home to keep an eye on you girls after Mum had, you know..."

Dad still had moments where he couldn't bring himself to say it and this was clearly one of them.

"I bet the grammar school isn't *that* good," I said, keen to change the subject.

"Come on, Liv," Dad said, almost pleading now. "All I ask is that you go and take a look. You don't have to commit to anything. Just look. I think you should at least be able to go and see what your options are having been offered a place there. You should be proud of yourself."

"It's not fair," I moaned. "Grace should have got in. I thought she would have done. If anything, I think we all expected that it would be her in the situation that I'm in right now."

Dad couldn't bring himself to say anything to that but we both knew I was right.

The awkward silence was broken when I noticed that Grace was stood there in the kitchen doorway.

"Have you been listening in on us?" I asked, a bit alarmed but not wanting to upset her. "I wouldn't blame you for it."

"A little," Grace said sheepishly.

She looked down at her pink fluffy slippers. All of us were still in our pyjamas. Nobody had thought to get dressed for the day, what with all the stress of opening those horrible envelopes from that rubbish grammar school. Who did they think they were, writing to us like this and ruining our Saturday morning?!

I felt myself starting to get angry again but before I had succumbed to it, Grace said something that shocked Dad and I.

"I want you to go and take a look at the grammar school, Liv," she said. "Like Dad said, just go and look at it. You can always turn it down if you don't want to go. But there's a chance that you might like it. You won't know until you try."

"But what about *you*?" I asked desperately.

It worried me to think that Grace wasn't being on the ball. Did she not know what she was saying?!

"Honestly," she said. "You owe it to Dad and you owe it to yourself. Besides, what kind of person would I be if I told you what to do?"

It felt strange to hear Grace say that. I often told *her* what to do. The one time that I wouldn't have minded *her* telling *me* what to do, she did the opposite. Grace was always so kind and passive. Gracious Grace. I wasn't so sure that I would be Gracious Olivia in her shoes (well, slippers!).

"Well done, Grace," said Dad as he signalled towards us both to come to him for a hug. "I'm proud of you both."

Chapter Ten

On Thursday afternoon after school, we all had a quick meal of chicken nuggets and chips before getting in the car to head off to the open evening at Linmore. Grace and I got in the car together apprehensively. When Dad needed to take one of us somewhere, the other always tagged along too. It was handy for Dad what with being a lone parent but also, Grace and I were always happy to go everywhere together. Even when Grace needed new shoes and I didn't, I would always go with her and Dad. Being twins didn't mean that our feet grew at the same rate!

Anyway, I was still hungry after having wolfed my dinner down and so Dad had given me a bag of sweets. Usually he was pretty big on healthy eating but this evening, he was being more relaxed about that. He clearly had other things on his mind. I offered Grace a sweet, taking it as an opportunity to make a peace offering to her, even though in the circumstances it felt a bit feeble.

"You know I like the red ones best," said Grace.

"Ah, but is it because I want to save the green ones for myself?" I said jokingly.

Although things felt a little tense between us, Grace and I wanted to be kind to each other. After all, it wasn't our fault that we were in this situation. It wasn't Dad's either. It was just one of those things.

The car journey didn't take long at all.

"See," said Dad. "We're nearly there now. I could easily take you to and from here every day, Liv. Not a motorway in sight either. This journey should be a breeze even during busier times."

I raised an eyebrow and looked across at Grace. I could tell that we were thinking the same thing: surely Dad was looking at Linmore grammar school with rose-tinted glasses.

I looked out of the window at all of the trees along the country road. I thought to myself about how daft Dad would look in a pair of glasses that actually had pink lenses. It made me snigger to myself. Dad must have caught sight of my expression in the rear-view mirror.

"Now then, Liv," he said. "I want you to give this a chance. You don't have to pretend to like it but I certainly don't want you to go into it assuming that you'll hate it. All I ask is that you at least take a look around with an open mind. Promise?"

"Ok Dad," I said. "I promise."

I wasn't even sure if I was telling him the truth or whether I was just saying what he wanted to hear because I would have felt guilty otherwise. Dad had put so much effort into this that it would have felt wrong to tell him that I wasn't going to try. As I thought more about it, I decided that I would try hard to be on my best behaviour this evening. There was no point in walking around and being in a huff about everything. Grace probably wouldn't want that anyway. She was often telling me that sometimes I was a bit on the loud side in public.

As Dad parked the car it was clear that we were in the right place. There were playing fields and several grand-looking buildings surrounding the car park. It looked incredibly posh compared to any school I had ever seen before, and much bigger than our primary school.

Once Dad had locked the car, he and Grace walked hand in hand towards the main reception building. I hung back and watched them.

"Come on, Liv," Dad said, turning back to me and almost pleading. "Give it a chance, eh?"

"I will," I insisted.

Grace smiled at me encouragingly. She was always so kind and patient with me even when things were difficult. It reminded me of how much it helped having her with me in primary school. If it wasn't for her and her calming influence, I would have probably got into even more fights – especially with stupid Gary.

As we all walked closer towards the building, the size of it became a bit intimidating. *Whatever,* I thought to myself. *Let's get this over and done with.*

It was in that moment that I decided I wouldn't like it here. It would probably be posh, snotty and *boring.* There would be nothing about it that could possibly make it worth being here without Grace.

A lady in a pink fluffy jumper and pointy-angled glasses looked up at us from behind the reception desk.

"Are you here for the open evening?" she asked.

"Yes," said Dad, walking towards the desk.

"Ok," said the lady.

She then handed him a map and started talking about where to go and about all the stuff that there was to see. There was too much to take in. Something about an art room and a tour guide and a performing arts block. How boring! My mind started to wander off even further until I heard the woman telling Dad about how the school was a sports academy.

Dad thanked the pink fluffy jumper lady and we followed the arrows that had been stuck up on the walls to show us where to go.

"Dad," I said. "What did that lady mean when she said about this place being a sports academy?"

"It means that Linmore is particularly well-known for their expertise and facilities in sport," said Dad. "They have football pitches and coaching, and a team that represents every year in the school."

"No way?!" I said, completely surprised. "I didn't even know that was a thing. At our school, they used to run a football club for a bit in year four but then the teacher who was doing it left at the end of term and it just kind of fizzled out."

"You might like it here, Liv," Dad said as he

waggled his ears playfully at me.

I didn't want him to be right but I would have been lying if I said I wasn't intrigued.

I looked over at Grace, worried about how she was feeling. It looked like she was working hard not to cry. I pretended not to notice. I didn't want to make her feel even more upset – that thing where someone asks if you're ok and then it's impossible to hold it all in.

****

We'd seen quite a bit of the school. It was quite a walk compared to the size of our primary school. Every time I thought we'd seen it all, there were more and more classrooms and more and more teachers to talk to. The maths room was boring but the teacher seemed nice enough. The English room was nothing special. The art room looked pretty cool, to be fair. I couldn't believe how many different instruments there were in the music room. It was the sports hall that really got my attention though.

"We've just got the trampolines out for fun really," said the P.E. teacher.

She had a sticker on her tracksuit top. *Mrs*

Cokerdale, it said.

"Wow!" I exclaimed as I looked around the hall. "You've got climbing holes in the wall. Do we get to have a go on those?"

"Yes, we do lessons with those," said Mrs Cokerdale. "We even have a climbing club. It's worth joining because it's for a couple of hours after school. It's probably going to be Wednesdays when it starts up in September. You'll get a bit longer than you would in a normal P.E. lesson so you'll get more time on the wall after you've spent the time putting the protective gear on."

"Wow!" I said again, genuinely impressed.

I hadn't expected Linmore to be this interesting up until now but suddenly, a thought crossed my mind.

"Hang on a minute," I said. "Don't the other secondary schools have trampolines and climbing walls and sports clubs?"

Dad looked pleased that I had thought to ask.

"They *might*," said Mrs Cokerdale. "But not in the abundance that we do."

"Oh," I said, disappointed that I was starting to like the thought of going to Linmore.

I looked over at Grace who was standing there quietly. That wasn't unusual for her but she certainly looked sad. Perhaps even a little bewildered. I desperately wanted to find something that would put me off from being impressed by this place.

"I bet you don't have a girls' football team here," I said, hoping a little that they wouldn't.

"We do," said Mrs Cokerdale, seeming happy that I was so interested. "In fact, we have several. Not only does each year in the school have a boys' football team, they also have a *girls'* football team too."

"Oh," I said.

I felt such a mixture of emotions in that moment. Linmore looked so fun but I still couldn't bear the thought of having to go there without Grace.

"Mrs Cokerdale," I said, hoping that I could use my rapport with her to my advantage. "My sister didn't pass the entry exam but I think she should still be able to come here in September. Honestly, she's really hard-working and she's much cleverer than I am."

Grace went red in the face.

"Olivia!" Dad snapped. "Don't be so rude. I know you care about Grace but that's not how it works."

"I see," said Mrs Cokerdale, suddenly looking very concerned. "I can see where you're coming from. You want to be at the same school as your twin sister, don't you?"

"Yes," I said, suddenly feeling like I was going to cry.

"I understand," said Mrs Cokerdale. "Moving up to secondary school can be scary enough for people who don't have a twin. I mean, think about it: twin or no twin, there are a lot of new things to get used to. Not only will there be more kids in your year, but you'll have a different teacher for each subject and you'll have to learn your way around the school pretty quickly. Someone always gets lost on the way to P.E. from the science block in the first term. What I'm getting at, is that it's normal to be worried, or even a bit scared."

I looked over at Grace. Admittedly, neither of us had thought about it like that before. We had been so wrapped up in wanting to stay together that we hadn't stopped to think about how maybe our concerns were similar to those of the other kids in year six – twin or no twin.

"You see," said Dad, smiling gratefully at Mrs Cokerdale and then looking back at Grace and I. "It's normal to have all kinds of worries. Moving from primary school to secondary school is a huge step for anyone – especially if you've been at the same small primary school since nursery. Think about it though girls, you've both been through so much. You can do this. You'll always be sisters and you'll always be together – even if you go to different secondary schools."

Grace started to cry. I took her aside to sit on the bench. I could see what Dad and Mrs Cokerdale were getting at, but it still hurt me to see Grace so upset. As Grace sobbed into my jumper, Dad continued to talk to Mrs Cokerdale. As he kept gesturing towards us, it was clear that he was telling the P.E. teacher about the situation with Grace and I.

"It's so unfair," Grace sobbed. "It's so bloody unfair."

"Hey!" I said, shocked and a little annoyed at her outburst. "You never swear like that. Don't *bloody* start now! I'm the one who swears."

Grace laughed a little. She knew I'd added that rude word because I wanted to make her laugh. I could tell that she appreciated it.

"Come on, Grace," I said. "It will be ok."

"Why will it?" she said, still sounding defeated.

"I don't know," I said honestly. "I guess it just will be."

"So you're just going to go to Linmore now?"

"I don't even know anymore," I said.

"Yeah, but it looks like you really like it here."

"But you *told* me to give it a chance," I said, exasperated.

"Yeah, but I didn't think that you'd actually *like* it here. You've never liked school that much anyway."

"So you didn't really mean it when you said that you wanted me to come to the open evening and give grammar school a chance?" I asked, the weight of the situation dawning on me heavily.

"I don't know," Grace said, crying really hard this

time. "I guess I just thought you'd look at this place and decide that it was rubbish or boring or whatever you'd normally call it, and then you'd tell Dad that you'd made the effort but it wasn't for you and that you wanted to go to the same secondary school as me."

"Is that what you wanted to happen?" I asked, tilting Grace's head so that she'd look me straight in the eyes.

"Yes," she said.

She darted her gaze away from mine. She seemed so ashamed.

"I'm not mad," I said. "Honestly, I'm just confused. I didn't think I'd like it here either and I'm really surprised that I do. In fact, I'm probably more surprised about it than you are. You *know* that I don't really like school. You *know* that I'm not really bothered about it and you *know* that I care about you more than anything else in the world."

The two of us sat quietly for a bit. I put my arm around Grace as she sniffled and tried to stop crying.

"Liv," she said, suddenly looking up at me and no longer trying to avoid my gaze. "What do you think

Mum would want us to do?"

"I think she'd want you to stop crying and to splash some cold water on your face," I said, desperately trying to lighten the mood for Grace's sake.

"No," said Grace. "I'm serious. What do you think Mum would want us to do about *this*?"

I thought about it for a moment. It was a good question and if I knew the answer to it, it would probably help us both. I was struggling to think straight though, what with everything that was going on. It wasn't just about the fact that Grace was crying – it was about the fact that I felt so guilty.

"I don't know," I said truthfully. "I wish I did. But I don't."

Dad was still talking to Mrs Cokerdale. She was nodding her head sympathetically. It dawned on me that it was probably doing him some good to be talking to another adult about Grace and I. He usually spent a lot of time on his own what with working from home, being so engrossed in his research and looking after us. It was nice to see him talking to someone who could hopefully offer an opinion. I was so confused by the whole situation that I didn't even know what I wanted Mrs

Cokerdale to be saying to Dad. How could anybody know what the best way forward would be?

****

On the car journey home, the three of us sat in silence. After the evening we'd all had, Dad didn't look as happy to be driving on the country roads as he had been earlier.

As I looked out of the window, I was glad that it was starting to get dark by now. I didn't want Grace to see that I was crying and I didn't want Dad to see either. Even though they both probably knew how sad I felt, I didn't want them to *see* it. I felt so guilty. It was horrible to know that I actually liked the look of Linmore. I had really gone to the open evening expecting that it would be easy to reject it. But it wasn't. It had actually been really exciting. If I didn't have Grace to worry about, I would have definitely said yes to it on the spot.

I started to think about how amazing it would be to play a good game of football without someone popping our ball, and without having to use piles of jumpers as goalposts – and with a proper referee and with proper training to work on some real skills. It would be amazing to play a proper game of football where people would actually pass the ball when it made sense to. It would be amazing to go to a school where I was actually interested in some of the lessons.

I could hear Grace sniffling next to me. For someone who wasn't coming down with a cold, her nose sounded really stuffy. She too was looking out of her window as if she didn't want me or Dad to see her face. She must have been crying too. Normally I would know just what to say and just what to do to cheer her up. I had always been brilliant at it. It made me so sad that in this situation, I had no idea what I could do to make her happy. Why was it that something that used to come so easily to us was now feeling so strained?

Chapter Eleven

The next morning, Grace stood quietly in front of the mirror as we got ready for school. She was taking longer than usual.

"Please don't ignore me," I begged. "It's not my fault that I liked Linmore."

"I know it's not your fault," she said. "And anyway, I'm not ignoring you. I'm just tired."

"Why?"

"I didn't sleep well last night."

That didn't come as a surprise to me. I had been so tired that I had dropped off to sleep straight away and had slept right through. It clearly hadn't been the same for Grace though.

"You could tell Dad you don't feel very well," I offered. "Then you could stay home for the day and go back to bed to catch up on some sleep."

"What good would that do?" Grace asked, a little annoyed.

"Because I don't like it when you're tired," I said. "It makes you grumpy."

"Oh," Grace snapped. "So it's all about you again is it?!"

"What?!" I said, hurt that she would even think that. "No. Not at all. I just want you to be ok."

"Yeah, well. I'm fine," said Grace, clearly not telling the truth.

She had never been this off with me before and I didn't know how to deal with it. There was a time when if I'd told her to stay home sick for the day, she'd have told Dad that she was too unwell to go to school. Dad had never questioned it because Grace was the sort of person who would push herself into doing something even if she had the flu. She was always trying to please other people and sometimes it had been necessary for me to step in and tell her that it was ok to take it easy.

I wondered if I would get into trouble less often at grammar school. I had occasionally told Dad that I needed the day off when I'd been completely fine, all because I wanted a day to relax.

Finally, Grace moved away from the mirror. She could barely look at me.

"Graaaaaace," I said playfully, trying to lighten the mood. "It's Friday today. Come on… Let's say we're sick so we can have the day at home together. Just us."

"I don't want to," said Grace.

"Why? You're tired."

"Maybe it's time that I started to think for myself a bit more," Grace insisted. "Why should I have a day off from school just because that's what *you* think I should do?"

There was nothing I could say to that. Maybe Grace was right.

"Maybe it's not about whether I'm tired or not," she continued. "Maybe it's time that I started to think for myself and make my own decisions a bit more."

"If you do that then we might as well go to separate secondary schools," I said.

"Actually," Grace said with a sigh. "You know how I didn't sleep well last night... Well, for most of it,

I was just staring ahead and thinking. Maybe it would do us both some good to have a bit more independence."

I had never heard Grace speak like that before. She had never even given any clues that she might have been feeling that way. Or if she had, I hadn't noticed.

"That's crazy," I said. "What about growing old together?"

"We'll do that anyway," said Grace, smiling at the thought. "We can still be *there* for each other without being *with* each other all of the time."

"Yeah, but doesn't that bother you?"

"I think maybe it used to, but I've been thinking about it a lot, Liv. We will always be there for each other but we're both very different people. And that's ok. I think that's a good thing."

"Yeah, but we're still close, right?"

"Of course we are. We always will be. But we should still be able to be ourselves without feeling guilty over it."

"So you're saying that you wouldn't be upset if we

didn't go to the same secondary school together?"

"I think I would be at first," Grace said as she gave my hand a reassuring squeeze. "But I think we'd be ok because we would get used to it. And anyway, if you really hated Linmore, you could always move to my school. I wouldn't want you to though, not really anyway. I want you to be happy. You're always saying how you don't like school so it would be amazing to see you go somewhere that you'd actually enjoy – hopefully anyway."

"You've really put a lot of thought into this."

"Of course. And if you really think about it, when we grow up, we'll both have different jobs. You're loud and I'm shy. You like sport and I like art."

"You're amazing," I said, giving Grace an enthusiastic hug.

She hugged me back just as tightly.

"Sisters forever, no matter what," she whispered in my ear.

Chapter Twelve

"Girls," Dad called up the stairs to us. "You're going to be late. You haven't even had your breakfast yet!"

I pulled away from Grace. We looked at each other and smiled. Usually Grace would have been the first one to panic if we were running late – not just for school but for anything. She hated to feel that she was getting things wrong. It had never bothered me. The way I saw it, if something mattered, it always got done in the end.

"Come on," I said kindly to Grace. "I'll help you. You can wear my jumper if you can't find yours."

"Your jumper has holes in the sleeves though!" Grace said, laughing.

She was right. My jumper had started to get tatty not long after Dad had purchased it brand-new at the start of year five. What started out as a small hole got bigger and bigger once I'd started to pull at it and twist my pencil or my thumb around the material. I had always been amazed at how Grace had managed to be so tidy.

"Right," I said. "Well, we'd better find your jumper."

I wasn't offended that Grace didn't want to borrow mine. As I started to look under her duvet in case she'd left it there, we heard Dad call up the stairs again.

"Girls! Come down for breakfast. It's getting ridiculously late."

We didn't want to just grab a bag of crisps on the way out of the door. The smell of a cooked breakfast coming from downstairs made it seem too inviting to miss out on. It was one of the advantages of Dad being a work-at-home parent.

"We're coming," I shouted downstairs before turning to talk to Grace. "Let's take our time today, Grace. I promise I'm not trying to be bossy or lazy. I just think that the last few days have been hard. We should be nice to ourselves. What's the big deal about being late for school, just this once?"

Grace looked relieved that I was telling her that it was going to be ok. It reminded me that even though we would be going to separate secondary schools, she still needed me. It wasn't just *her* who needed *me* though – it was *me* who needed *her*. I gave her another hug, charged out of the bedroom door, and then thundered down the stairs, happy that we had decided what we were going to do. It felt like a weight had been lifted.

Grace followed downstairs behind me, a little slower but not through being worried about anything. As I turned back to wait for her to come into the kitchen with me, she still looked sleepy.

"Dad, Dad, Dad!" I sang as I jumped happily into the kitchen.

"Better late than never," he said, smiling as he carefully put a fried egg on both of our plates.

"Morning," said Grace.

"You're both running pretty late now. Did one of you oversleep?" Dad asked, concern in his voice.

"Kind of," I said. "It's not that one of us overslept. It's that Grace didn't sleep well at all. Well, that, and we've just had a big talk."

"We needed it," Grace said, looking as relieved as I felt.

"Oh," said Dad, with one eyebrow raised. "Well, you both seem happy about it. Is it good news?"

Dad looked at us expectantly. He seemed hopeful. I couldn't tell if he was hopeful that we were going to tell him what he wanted to hear, or whether he was just pleased that Grace and I seemed happier than we had been for a while.

Grace yawned. She looked like she was going to fall asleep at any moment.

"Are you ok?" Dad asked her. "You look very tired."

"I am tired," she said. "Can I stay home today? I feel like I need to go back to bed."

"Of course you can," Dad said. "Are you still hungry?"

"A little," Grace said sheepishly.

It was as if she felt that she needed to be unwell in order to stay home from school.

I thought about whether or not I wanted to go to school today. I wasn't tired but I wouldn't have minded having a day just to hang out and relax. It made me wonder whether the other kids at

Linmore would be total swots or if they too were the kind who liked to take a day off every now and then. If I could get into grammar school without too much effort, then maybe there would be all kinds of kids there. I was starting to think that it would be exciting to meet them.

As Grace pushed her beans around her plate, trying to decide whether or not she actually felt like eating, I figured that I should tell Dad about the talk we'd just had upstairs.

"Grace had a bad night's sleep because she was upset and worried about the whole school thing," I said.

"I thought that might have been it," said Dad.

"But we've decided what we want to do now. It's good news, I promise," I said.

"Oh?" said Dad.

"Yeah," I said. "We've decided that we're both going to run away and live on a tropical island and live like princesses and build a fortress so tall and so sturdy that nobody can get in and nobody can make either of us go to school ever again."

Grace sniggered as she ate her bacon, and even

Dad couldn't hide his amusement. I had always felt the need to break the tension between the three of us whenever anything felt awkward.

"I hope you know how to do your own washing then," Dad joked.

"No thank you," I said, squirming at the thought of having to do all the other boring jobs in the house, well fortress.

"We're going to go to different schools, Dad," Grace piped up.

"Really?" he asked.

"Yes," I butted in, wanting to give Grace some time to just relax. "After having talked about it together, it's hard to explain it maybe, but we just want each other to be happy. We have decided that we will always be together – going to different secondary schools can't take that away from us. Grace will always be my twin and I will always be there for her. It's exactly the same the other way around as well."

"That's a great way of looking at it," said Dad. "I'm relieved but more than that, I'm *proud* of you both. You can both be there for each other in life no matter what it throws at you. And who knows, maybe you'll have similar situations later on as you experience new things."

"Like what?" I asked.

"Oh, I don't know," said Dad, trying to think of some examples off the top of his head. "Things like where you might want to live in the future. One of you could be offered an amazing job that is miles and miles away."

"Wow!" I said. "I'd never thought of that."

I looked across to Grace to see if what Dad had just said had upset her. Thankfully, she looked calm.

"Maybe in the long run, it's a good thing that you have both gone through something like this now," said Dad. "I think it has encouraged you both to grow up a bit. Not that I want my princesses to grow up too fast, of course, but you know, it's experiences like this that will prepare you for other things in life. Having a twin must be so special and unique and I think it's lovely that you care about each other so much. I think Mum would be proud of you both."

There were times when talking about Mum felt too painful. Perhaps to all of our surprise though, this didn't feel like one of them. It felt nice to think about what Mum would have said about all of this.

"Do you wish you had a twin, Dad?" I asked.

I was suddenly wondering if he felt lonely at times. Even though he seemed happy to spend lots of time on his own, maybe he still felt lonely.

"I think one of me is enough," Dad said, waggling his ears comically. "Now then, Grace, you're staying home today. That's fine. I want you to relax. Have a sleep or watch some TV while I work in my office. Do whatever you need to do."

"Will you write me a letter to give to Mrs Greenwood to explain why I'm late?" I asked.

Both Grace and Dad looked surprised that I still wanted to go to school. Normally I would have taken advantage of the situation and asked if I could have the day at home too. This time though, I wanted to go to school. I wanted to prove to myself that I didn't need to do the same thing as Grace when given a choice about it.

"Of course," said Dad. "I'll get that done while you finish your breakfast and then we'll head off."

"Thanks Dad," I said.

Chapter Thirteen

Dad walked with me to class and when he explained why I was late and why Grace was absent, Mrs Greenwood was very understanding. Mrs Greenwood was alright really and I would probably miss her after primary school. Although there had been plenty of times where she had told me off – especially in year six – she had always been fair.

The rest of the morning was quiet and relaxing. It was a bit boring without Grace sitting next to me but more than that, I was happy to think that she would be catching up on some much-needed sleep. Or even just sitting around in her pyjamas and watching cartoons.

By lunch break, things were even more boring without Grace. But it didn't matter. I didn't want to play football with the boys anymore. I'd had enough of them not playing it properly. I'd had enough of everyone fighting around the ball. I wasn't in the mood for a scuffle. It wasn't because

I was upset or in a bad mood, it was because I was looking forward to taking sport more seriously at Linmore. It would be amazing to play a proper game, with a referee.

As I sat on the wall enjoying the warm breeze of the day, I looked up to see Gary walking towards me. As usual, he had Craig and Tom with him. I tried to make it look like I was busy but there was nobody else around. There wasn't much I could do to make it look like I hadn't noticed him.

"Where's Grace?" he asked in a mocking tone of voice.

"She's absent today," I said.

"Yeah, but why?"

"Not that it's any of your business," I said. "But she's not very well today."

"So I guess you've got no mates to hang out with now," Gary said.

Craig and Tom laughed at Gary's stupid comment. Sometimes it was hard to tell if they found him genuinely funny, or if they would have laughed at anything just because they wanted to impress him.

"What's it to you?" I asked, not really caring about Gary's – or anyone else's – opinion.

"It's just that you look pretty daft sat there on your own," Gary said.

There had been a time in year six where by now I would be facing Gary square on – angry and ready to fight. It felt so pointless now though. Why would I want to fight someone whose opinion meant nothing to me anyway?

"Well, maybe I do," I said with a shrug. "I'm not really bothered to be honest with you."

"You're so weird," Craig chimed in. "You're not even playing football. Maybe nobody likes you anymore."

"Yeah," Tom said, laughing. "Maybe people only pretend to like you when really it's just Grace they like."

Gary laughed at this.

I was amazed at how indifferent I felt towards the three of them. They were clearly trying to get a reaction out of me. They may as well have been reeling off a list of what they'd just eaten for lunch though. Nothing they said had any meaning or relevance to me anymore.

"Look," I said, keen to level with all of them. "I can see what you're getting at. You're trying to wind me up and it's not working. You *could* keep at it. Maybe it would even work, who knows? But really, this is just boring now. You're just saying a load of stuff for the sake of it."

"Are you telling me to shut up?" Gary demanded, rolling up his sleeves and edging nearer towards me, clearly wanting a fight.

I didn't stand up. I sort of wanted to – just to be on the safe side, but I knew that would have just given Gary exactly what he was looking for.

"I'm not telling you to shut up," I said, keeping my voice calm and controlled. "I'm saying that I don't want to fight."

"You're mega weak," Craig said, trying to help Gary get a reaction out of me.

"What's weak about not wanting to get into trouble?" I asked.

My question must have given them all food for thought because they looked at each other, slightly confused.

"Think about it," I continued. "If we get into a fight, all that will happen is that we'll have to go to Mrs Greenwood's office to get moaned at. Then we'll have to take a letter home. Why don't we just *not* have a fight and save ourselves the trouble?"

Although Gary looked impressed with what I was saying, he still seemed like he wasn't going to leave me alone just yet.

"I bet you'd fight if you thought Grace needed you to. Too bad she's not in today," he said.

I didn't say anything to this. I stayed silent and looked the other way, hoping that Gary and his cronies would go away. I wasn't upset at his comment, not at all. If anything, it had given me something to think about.

"You're strange," said Gary, keen to get the last word in before he signalled to Craig and Tom to follow his lead and walk away.

Once they had turned the corner to head off to the other end of the playground, I sighed in relief. I reached into my pocket to get a packet of mints out. It was nice to be on my own again. Still though, some of Gary's comments made my thoughts whirl around in my head.

Would I really have been more likely to get into a fight if I thought it would protect Grace? A lot of the time, was getting into trouble more about how I wanted to look out for her?

Well, maybe it was, but I couldn't be sure either way. The idea bounced around in my head for the rest of the afternoon. Maybe there would be more advantages to us going to different secondary schools that we had first thought. Maybe it would be good for me to not be so on-edge and worried about looking out for Grace all the time. In the same way, maybe it would be good for her to find her own voice if someone started giving her any trouble. Of course, I'd always be there for her and I'd always want to know she was ok. That feeling would *never* go away. I knew that. I had probably known it since the day we were born. Still though, it felt inspiring to think that Grace and I could both grow, not just together, but apart as well.

When the school day was nearly over, I thought about telling Mrs Greenwood what Gary and his two sad little followers had said to me in the playground at lunchtime. I thought it would be good for her to know that Gary was still trying to cause trouble and that it wasn't me who she needed to keep a watchful eye on. I decided not to bother though. Olivia Radley doesn't tell on people. It was more than that though. I figured that whether it was

Gary, his lame little mates or someone else, there would always be *somebody* out there to cause trouble. It wouldn't make sense to dob them in all the time. I didn't want to be *that* kid. No, I knew that I could stick up for myself without getting into fights. Grace had never been in a fight in her life and she seemed perfectly happy about it. I could learn from Grace without having her next to me at every turn.

As the bell rang to signal that it was home time, I gathered my things and headed happily out of the classroom and down the corridor. I was looking forward to getting home and telling Grace about my day. Not only that, but it would be nice to see her looking better for having had the day off.

Chapter Fourteen

As soon as I got home I crept up the stairs. I was bursting to see how Grace was doing – and if she'd managed to catch up on some sleep. Not only that, but I wanted to tell her about my day.

I opened the door slowly so as not to make it creak. Grace had always been a lighter sleeper than me.

"You can come in, you know," she said.

"I didn't want to wake you up. I thought you might be asleep," I said.

"Nope, all done," she said. "I slept for a few hours once you'd gone but I've been awake all afternoon."

It looked like she'd had a nice day. She was sat on the floor with her pencils and gel pens, all arranged neatly in front of her. She was working on another drawing of a flower. She was great at drawing flowers. Next to the flower, there was a cute little bunny rabbit looking up at the petals in admiration. I felt just like how that bunny felt as I looked at Grace. She was so good at making her art look like the things that they were supposed to look like. Most people, even adults, would struggle to draw something better.

"That one needs to go on the wall," I said as I pointed at the work in progress.

"Thank you," Grace said sweetly as she put down the pencil in her hand to focus on me. "Did it go ok today? Did you get in trouble for being late? Was Mrs Greenwood ok with me being absent?"

"Yes, no and yes," I said with a smile. "Now then, now it's the weekend, are you going to stop worrying? Please? Just a little bit?"

"I think so," said Grace, a little reluctantly. "Kind of."

"What do you mean, *kind of*?"

"Dad found out that there's an open evening at Cresswood on Monday. That's the secondary school that I'll be going to."

"That's great," I said. "That's nothing to worry

"about."

"I'm a bit nervous," Grace said shyly.

"Well you would be. That's normal," I said, wanting to reassure her. "You know how nervous I was before I went for a look around at Linmore."

"I hope I like it at Cresswood."

"You will," I said.

"How do you know?"

"Because you've always been better at fitting in than I have. Because you've always been good at behaving and concentrating and getting your work done and doing as you're told."

"That's true. But what if I find it hard to make friends?"

"You won't. You're lovely. A few of the girls asked me today where you were."

"What did you tell them?"

"I told them that you got eaten by a monster," I said, laughing too hard at my own silliness. "Yeah, and they gave me that same weird look that you're giving me now. That's how I know you're going to be fine when you go to a different secondary school. I swear you're not as weird as me."

"You're not weird."

"Gary thinks I am. And Craig. And Tom. And all of the girls. I don't care. What they think doesn't matter to me anymore."

"How come?" asked Grace, genuinely surprised.

"Well," I said. "Most of them will be going to a different school, but more than that, I *am* weird, Grace. Come on, just be honest about it. It doesn't bother me."

"Am *I* weird?" Grace asked, sounding a little worried.

"Maybe," I said, laughing a little. "Some people find us both weird as soon as they meet us – simply because we're twins. I still think you're not as weird as me though."

Grace looked relieved.

"And anyway," I continued. "The world would be super boring if everyone was the same. Even *we* wouldn't want to be the same as each other really, would we?"

"I agree," said Grace.

She carefully started to tidy up her art stuff. The very fact that she was always so careful to put everything back so neatly in order of colour and size was enough to remind me of our differences. Even if I'd had a talent for art, I would just want to cram everything back in the box any old way – just to get the job over and done with. Tidying up is so boring and yet Grace had never seemed to mind doing it. In fact, she even seemed to take a lot of pride in it. *Maybe she is the weird one after all*, I thought to myself.

"So what's happening with the open evening at Cresswood?" I asked. "Do you want me to go with you?"

"I hadn't thought that far ahead," said Grace.

"Good," I said enthusiastically. "That means that you're not worrying about going in on your own."

"Well, maybe I am. Just a little though. I promise."

"That's normal," I said. "I'll tell you what else is normal as well."

"What?" she asked.

"Being hungry and wanting chips for dinner on a Friday!" I sang out. "Shall we ask Dad if he'll take us to McDonald's?"

Grace often tried to discourage me from asking Dad to take us to McDonald's. Even though she loved the food there as much as I did, she didn't want to upset him, knowing that he preferred us to eat lots of vegetables instead.

I stood with my hands on my hips, tapping my foot. I knew exactly what Grace was thinking and I let her know as much by sticking my tongue out at her. She knew what I was getting at. It was one of those moments where we could understand each other without speaking.

"Ok," she said happily. "It'll be nice to go there, the three of us together."

With that, we raced down the stairs to go and find Dad.

Chapter Fifteen

The weekend flew past and Monday evening came around soon enough. The car ride to Cresswood didn't take long at all. The place looked just as big and just as intimidating on the outside as Linmore had when the three of us had gone to the open evening there.

"Are you sure you don't want me to come in with you?" I said to Grace as she got out of the car.

"Honestly, it's fine," she said.

I could tell she meant it too. She didn't look worried at all. She even looked like she was looking forward to finding out more about where she would be going in September. I was pleased for her, especially because I didn't want the fact that I had got into Linmore to overshadow her own talents. Nothing would ever make me question Grace's intelligence. I still felt that she was smarter than me. She may not have scored as highly on some stupid entry test, but she was often the more mature out of the two of us – even though she was born a few minutes after me.

"I'm not sure how long we'll be gone, Liv," said Dad. "There's a bottle of water in the bag next to your seat if you need one."

"Thanks Dad," I said.

As I watched Dad and Grace walk away from the car, I settled down to play a video game. I didn't feel nervous or worried for Grace. I knew she'd be fine. I could sense it.

****

I didn't know how long I had been sat in the car for. Whenever I played video games, it was always so easy to lose track of the time. It could have been twenty minutes or it could have been an hour. The time hadn't dragged. And most importantly of all, when I looked up to the sound of running feet pounding towards the car, it was Grace. She was beaming from ear to ear and she motioned energetically for Dad to hurry up. She looked like she was bursting to tell me something big.

As soon as the car door flung open, Grace jumped in to sit next to me. Her look of enthusiasm was contagious and I knew I would struggle to get a word in. Good. It was nice to just listen to her sometimes and this was one of those moments.

"It was brilliant, Liv," she said.

She sounded optimistic. I knew she wasn't putting it on to humour me either. It was moments like this in which I could read her like a book.

"It was great," she said. "I'm over the moon about it."

"It's only school, Grace," I said, slightly amused.

"Yeah, but you should have seen the art room," she said. "It was brilliant and the teachers there seem really nice. We looked at lots of other parts of the school too, but it's the art room that I'm excited about. They had all kinds of paints and massive canvases and the teachers were telling me about how I'd be welcome to go there at lunch time – as long as I tidy up afterwards."

"That will be easy for you because you love tidying," I joked.

Grace knew that I was only messing about. It was impossible to hide how happy I felt for her.

"I'm looking forward to it," she said. "The art that

is, and the school overall. It looks ok and everyone there seems nice enough, even though the size of the place is *huge* compared to our primary school."

"I guess that means we'll both be meeting lots of new people in September," I said.

"And don't either of you be worried about it," Dad chipped in as he reached around to fasten his seatbelt. "Well, it's ok to be a *bit* nervous, of course. That's normal. But just don't go worrying yourselves silly over the summer holidays. No more sleepless nights please."

"Nahhh, we'll be fine, Dad," I said. "There's loads of stuff that Grace and I can get up to in the holidays. We might even want a break from each other by the time it comes to September."

"It's true, Dad," Grace piped up, enjoying getting in on the joke.

"Seriously though," I said. "It will be nice to come home and tell each other about what our new schools are like."

"I think you'll both thrive," said Dad. "Each in your own and special unique way. There's a lot to look forward to."

****